EVE BUNTING

A Picnic in October

Illustrated by Nancy Carpenter

HARCOURT, INC.

Orlando Austin New York San Diego Toronto London

Printed in Singapore

Library of Congress Cataloging-in-Publication Data
Bunting, Eve, 1928–
A Picnic in October/by Eve Bunting; illustrated by Nancy Carpenter.
p.   cm.
Summary: A boy finally comes to understand why his grandmother insists
that the family come to Ellis Island each year to celebrate Lady Liberty's birthday.
ISBN 0-15-201656-2
1. Statue of Liberty (New York, N.Y.)—Juvenile fiction.   [1. Statue of Liberty
(New York, N.Y.)—Fiction.   2. Emigration and immigration—Fiction.
3. Italian Americans—Fiction.]   I. Carpenter, Nancy, ill.   II. Title.
PZ7.B91527Lab   1999
[E]—dc21   98-20044

R Q P O N M L K J

Printed in Singapore

The illustrations in this book were done in acrylic paint on paper.
The display type was set in Latiennne Medium Swash.
The text type was set in Aries.
Color separations by Bright Arts Graphics Pte. Ltd., Singapore
Printed and bound by Tien Wah Press, Singapore
Production supervision by Stanley Redfern and Ginger Boyer
Designed by Linda Lockowitz

To Barry Moreno, Librarian, Liberty Island,
who has so much knowledge to share
—E. B.

To Carol
—N. C.

Dad and Mom and I take the bus to Battery Park. We're carrying the stuff for the birthday picnic. Mom has the cake.

It's October 28, bright and sharp and cold. Really cold.

"Why do we always have to do this?" I ask Mom. "A picnic in October! It's dumb!"

"This is the way Grandma wants it," Mom says.

And that's the end of it.

When we get to Battery Park, I see Grandma right away. She's wearing her bright green coat. The wind ruffles the fake fur collar around her neck. Grandpa's with her, and Uncle Joe and Aunt Louise, and my cousins, Rosa and Mike. They're loaded with picnic stuff, too.

We all hug and kiss.

Grandpa reaches inside his overcoat and gives Rosa and Mike and me licorice sticks. He keeps a row of them in his top jacket pocket the way other people keep pens. He's wearing his usual black hat. Rosa says he wears that hat to bed. But I don't think so.

"We'd better hurry and get in the ferry line," Aunt Louise says.
I look at the line and I can see we're going to have a long wait.
We stomp our feet and blow on our hands.
Across on the island, the Statue of Liberty stands, green and gleaming.
"She was all spruced up a few years back," Grandma says. "She sure looks good for her age."

Grandpa strokes Grandma's cheek. "Like you, sweetheart," he says. Grandpa can be really soppy.

Mike's holding the cake now, in its see-through container. "Remember last year? Remember trying to get all the candles to fit on here?"

I nod. "We only brought ten this time. Grandma says when you're real old, you don't care about having one for every year, anyway."

A woman with a thick braid of black hair pulls at my arm. She's wearing a long colored skirt that brushes the ground beneath her coat. There's a little girl with her and a man in loose white pants that flap in the wind. The woman tugs harder on my arm and points to the ferry, which is chugging away from the dock. She's talking to me and I don't understand the words, but I can see she's worried.

"What's she saying?" Mike asks me.

"I think she's worried because the boat's gone," I say.

I smile at the woman. "It's OK," I say. "There'll be another boat." I point at the ferry, then at the end of the line, then back at the ferry. I make a turn-around sweep with my arm. "Another will come."

She smiles and nods, and I can tell she understands and feels better.

Mike sniggers. "Man! You looked like a third-base umpire, waving your arms like that. You looked like a dork."

"Don't be rude, Mike," Grandma says. "Tony was being kind. You are *not* being kind."

I wiggle my ears at Mike and that makes him laugh, so Grandma gives him another disapproving stare.

The next ferry comes and we manage to squeeze on. I watch for the woman and her family, but they don't make it onto this boat. I hope they don't give up.

The grown-ups rush inside where it's warm, but we just put our stuff in there and run to the front of the boat. We pretend to throw up over the railing. There's nobody up at the bow, so we spit into the wind and see who it blows back on. Spit is lucky.

Liberty Island is coming closer.
The statue is getting bigger.

We straggle off at the dock, lugging the picnic stuff.

The island is crowded, but Dad finds a grassy spot and the grown-ups spread the blankets. The three of us run around.

"That's the Verrazano Bridge," I say.

Mike points. "There's Brooklyn." Brooklyn is where Mike and Rosa live.

Sailboats dip into the wind.

"There's Ellis Island," Rosa says in a reading kind of way. "Seventeen million immigrants entered the United States of America through Ellis Island. We learned that in school."

"You told us last year," I say.

Rosa's offended. "So?"

"Tony! Rosa! Mike!" Dad calls.

"Chow time," Mike says.

We all sit on the blankets except for Grandma and Grandpa. We brought the folding chairs for them.

There's a ton of food.

Our paper plates keep blowing away. We try throwing them back, like Frisbees, but the wind carries them in the other direction and we have to chase them again. We dump them in the trash. The ginger ale is so cold it burns my throat.

Lady Liberty gazes down on us with her calm, old eyes.

"You'd think she'd get tired, holding her arm up like that," Rosa says.

I groan. "Give us a break! She's not *real*!"

Grandma frowns. "She's not alive, if that's what you mean. But she's certainly real. And so is what she stands for."

She smiles at Grandpa. "It's time for the birthday. Light the candles, Luigi."

The wind blows out every match Grandpa lights. The candles lean toward Staten Island and the wicks get stuck in the frosting. We straighten them and make a hands barrier between them and the wind.

It's a miracle they stay lit while Dad lifts the cake for Grandma to blow them out. They go with one huff when we take our hands away.

"Brava, Bella!" Grandpa cries. "Brava" means "you're wonderful" in Italian. "Bella" means "beautiful." Grandpa is being soppy again.

Dad refills our paper cups and we stand to face Lady Liberty. "Happy Birthday!" we shout. We touch cups and drink.

"When I came from the old country," Grandma says, "I came out here and I said: 'Thank you, Lady Liberty. Thank you for taking me in.' I spoke in Italian, of course, but she understands all languages. 'This is America, and I am here and I am a part of it,' I thought."

She says this every time. Grandma thinks the statue is such a big deal.

Grandpa leads us in the Happy Birthday song to Lady Liberty and then Grandma begins to recite the famous words:

"Give me your tired, your poor,
Your huddled masses yearning to breathe free . . ."

There's more. She recites them here on Lady Liberty's birthday every single year. Not much wonder she knows them by heart. Rosa does, too. She's very uppity about it.

Grandma blows kisses, so we feel we have to. I sincerely hope no one is watching.

After that we pack up what's left of the picnic and walk to the back part of the island, called the mall. There's a birthday program there, too. A brass band is playing. The Veterans of Foreign Wars are having a parade. What a party Lady Liberty's having! We stay for a while, and then we come back around.

I see the woman in her long, bright skirt with the man and the little girl.
I grin. "Look! There she is! They made it!" I say. "They got the ferry."
Grandma nods. "I bet they're new Americans. I know how they feel."
They are staring up at the statue, and then the man says something and
they hold hands and bow their heads. The way they stand, so still, so
respectful, so . . . so peaceful, makes me choke up. Maybe they've come to the
end of a long journey. Farther than just from Battery Park to Liberty Island

I put my arm around Grandma and hold my cup of ginger ale up to Lady Liberty. I think I'm seeing her for the very first time. "Brava, Bella!" I say. "Happy birthday!" And I don't care who's watching.